Everyone Loves
TYTY

A Little Boy Learns the Lessons of Life through Prayer and Proverbs

Antonett Kerr

Trilogy Christian Publishers
A Wholly Owned Subsidary of Trinity Broadcasting Network
2442 Michelle Drive
Tustin, CA 92780

Cover design by: Cornerstone Creative Solutions

For information, address Trilogy Christian Publishing
Rights Department, 2442 Michelle Drive, Tustin, Ca 92780.
Trilogy Christian Publishing/ TBN and colophon are trademarks of Trinity Broadcasting Network.

For information about special discounts for bulk purchases, please contact Trilogy Christian Publishing.

Manufactured in the United States of America

10 9 8 7 6 5 4 3 2 1

Library of Congress Cataloging-in-Publication Data is available.

ISBN 978-1-64773-887-7 (Print Book)
ISBN 978-1-64773-888-4 (ebook)

Dedication

This humble book is dedicated to my Lord and Savior, Jesus Christ, who has been my rock and the center of my life. Also to my mother, Winnifred Kerr, who has taught me about Jesus all my life. Thank you, Mom, for the best gift of all.

This book belongs to:

_____

Contents

Acknowledgments

I want to express my special thanks and appreciation to all my adorable siblings who are always there for me, Sharon, Carleen, Opal, Keisha, and Everol, who have spent countless hours listening to my stories with joy and laughter. Also to my precious Monica and Rohan, with whom I had the pleasure of working and sharing timeless, precious, fun memories. Again, to all my nieces and nephews, Justin, Chadwick, Caitlin, Victoria, Gavrielle, and Gabrielle, thank you for your contagious laughter.

Tyty Chooses God's Wisdom

Tyty was eight years old. He had curly hair and big brown eyes, and he loved to laugh.

Everyone loved Tyty, even though Tyty was always getting in trouble!

Early one morning, he woke up and rolled out of bed. The morning dew was still on the grass as he looked through his window. The entire neighborhood, along with his family, was still sleeping.

Tyty wanted to go outside and play, but there was no one in sight.

What should I do? he wondered. *Should I disobey my mother and father and go outside to play? Or should I listen to them and obey?*

I wonder what God would say about this? he thought. He knelt beside his bed and folded his hands in prayer. His Sunday school class had been studying Proverbs, and he liked them very much.

Proverbs 1:7-8 says that the fear of the Lord is the beginning of knowledge, he remembered. *But fools despise wisdom and instruction. He also recalled, "My son, hear the instruction of your father, and forsake not the law of your mother."*

As Tyty prayed, he realized that it was very dangerous to leave the house alone. So he obeyed his parents and went back to bed, and he had a wonderful dream. He dreamed that he went to heaven and was playing baseball with God and the angels. He hit seven home runs and was so happy that he rolled all over the baseball field!

Knock, knock, knock! Tyty's mother was banging on his bedroom door. "It's time for your breakfast," she called out.

Tyty woke up and said, "It feels so good to obey my parents. Thank you, God!"

A Soft Answer Turns Away Wrath

The sun was peeking out its round face at 7:00 in the morning. Tyty got ready for school, ate his entire breakfast, and waved goodbye to his parents. Then he ran to catch the school bus.

In class, he and his best friend, Bob, studied very hard together, always trying to get As. When the bell rang, Bob said to Tyty, "Let's have lunch together in the cafeteria."

"Sounds good to me," Tyty answered. But while they were eating their lunch, Sean, the class bully, came up to them and said, "I saw you two looking funny at me in math class. I'm going to smash your faces after school today." Then he walked away.

"We weren't looking at you!" said Tyty.

"I'm not afraid of him," Bob added. "If he touches me, I'm going to show him what I am made of."

"Let's not fight him," said Tyty. "Let's stay calm and polite."

"I'm not sure I can do that," said Bob.

"Let's try," answered Tyty. "The Bible tells us that we can turn away anger by staying calm and speaking nicely. Proverbs 15:1 says, 'A soft answer turns away wrath, but grievous words stir up anger.'"

The school bell rang, and the day was over. As the boys were walking to the bus, Sean stopped them and again said, "Why were you looking at me in math class?" Then he grabbed Bob by his collar, but Bob got away.

So he went after Tyty, who wisely said, "I would *never* look at you funny! I think you are a very nice person and very smart. Would you like to have lunch with me?"

"You really like me?" said Sean.

"God says you are beautifully and wonderfully made," Tyty replied.

"Then I can be your friend?"

"Yes! Would you like to play baseball with me tomorrow?"

"Well… I have to ask my grandma," Sean said.

That night, before going to bed, Tyty prayed:

"Dear God,

A soft answer does turn away wrath. Thank You for showing me that grievous words do stir up anger, and thank You for my new friend. He isn't a bully any more; his name is Sean, and he is now a good friend to Bob and me. They apologized and made up. One more thing, God? Thanks for making me wise. I love you more than I can say! Good night."

Guess Who's Watching?

It was a bright and sunny day. Tyty's parents were leaving for a meeting in the city. Before they left, they told him, "We'll be back for dinner. Please take care of your little sister, Cindy. No fighting, and listen to your babysitter! Oh, and one more thing…*do not leave the yard.*"

"Okay, Mom," Tyty replied. "I hear you, and I'll obey."

Tyty and Cindy played jumprope for a while. Then Cindy announced, "I'm bored! Let's go over to the neighbor, Mr. Curly Nose's, yard and play jumprope with his clothes that are hanging on the line." (Cindy and Tyty called their neighbor Mr. Curly Nose because his nose turned up.)

"Are you crazy?" Tyty said. "We'll get in big trouble! Mom and Dad said not to leave the yard."

Just then, the babysitter came to the window and called out, "Are you kids okay? Do you want some lemonade?"

"No, ma'am," Tyty and Cindy said together. "We're fine."

"Listen, Tyty," Cindy said. "We can stand at the fence. When the wind blows Mr. Curly Nose's pants off the line, we can grab them. We won't be leaving the yard, so we won't get in trouble."

Cindy ran to the fence, and Tyty chased after her. The wind blew Mr. Curly Nose's pants to the edge of the fence, and Cindy caught them. Tyty was furious! He tried to grab the pants from Cindy, but she hung on with a tight grip.

"Give me those pants!" Tyty yelled.

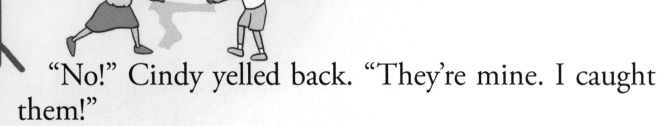

"No!" Cindy yelled back. "They're mine. I caught them!"

Tyty and Cindy played tug-of-war with the pants, back and forth and back and forth. Then suddenly, the pants ripped in two!

"Oops," said Cindy. "Look what you did!"

"Look what I did? This is *your* fault; what should we do?"

"I've got an idea," said Cindy. "We can put the pants in the bottom of the garbage and pretend nothing happened. We won't get in trouble because no one will see us. So, no big deal, right? They're just old pants, and they belong in the garbage anyway."

"Oh no, Cindy," said Tyty. "That doesn't sound right. And it's not honest."

But Cindy took the ripped pants and stuffed them into the bottom of the garbage can. "See?" she said to Tyty. "No one is watching."

Tyty thought for a minute and then said, "Someone *is* watching, and He is not pleased with us. As it says in Proverbs 15:3, 'The eyes of the Lord are in every place, beholding the evil and the good.' I have to tell Mom and Dad when they get home."

That evening, when their parents arrived home, Tyty confessed to what he and Cindy had done. They both were punished; Cindy and Tyty had to give up their allowances until Mr. Curly Nose's pants were paid for. And Tyty and Cindy had to go to Mr. and Mrs. Curly Nose and apologize in person!

Friends

On a calm Sunday evening, Tyty and his family sat in the dining room having dinner, which was delicious (Tyty's mother was a very good cook).

"Hey, Mom and Dad," said Tyty, "Did you know that there's a new family in the neighborhood? They're called the Buds."

"How do you know that?" asked Tyty's father.

"Well, the name Bud is written on their mailbox. I saw the movers; they were moving furniture from a big trailer truck into the house. I think they have a son named Joshua."

"How do you know that?" said Tyty's mother.

"I heard Mrs. Bud say 'Be careful. Joshua,'" he replied. "Please, can we go and meet them?"

"I don't know, Tyty," she said. "Maybe we shouldn't bother them."

"Did you know that my Sunday school teacher told us to always show ourselves friendly?" said Tyty. "She told us that, in Proverbs 18:24 it says that a man who has friends must show himself friendly, and there is a friend that sticks closer than a brother."

Tyty's parents took his advice, and his mom baked a batch of chocolate chip cookies and corn muffins for the Buds.

"Okay, Tyty," said his father. "Let's go welcome our new neighbors."

The whole family went to greet the Buds, who were happy to meet them, especially Tyty. They planned play dates with Joshua, who played baseball in the backyard with Bob and Sean. And the parents became good friends—all thanks to Tyty!

Love

It had been a wonderful year for Tyty. He had learned many lessons and made new friends. Tyty loved God, so he decided to write Him a letter with words straight from his heart:

"Dear God,

Thank You for teaching me your ways and directing my every step. In Proverbs 3:5-6, it says, 'Trust in the Lord with all your heart and do not lean to your own understanding. In all your ways I acknowledge him and he shall direct your path."

So, God, here is my thank-you list:

1. Thank You for being a kind and loving Father.
2. Thank You for the delicious meals You provide for us to eat.
3. Thank You for a good night's sleep.

4. Thank You for the world so sweet, for the beautiful flowers and trees and animals, too.
5. Thank You for the air we breathe.
6. Thank You for my friends and family, especially Mom, Dad, and my little sister, Cindy.
7. Thank You, God, for loving and filling me with wisdom, love, knowledge, and understanding. I love you with all my heart!

Love always,

Tyty

P.S. Good night!"